Jack and the Bean Soup

Mark Pendergrast

Illustrations by
Robert Waldo Brunelle, Jr.

Nature's Face Publications
2010

For information on books by Mark Pendergrast, or to contact him, see www.markpendergrast.com.

For information on the cartoons and art of Robert Waldo Brunelle, Jr., or to contact him, see www.mrbrunelle.com.

Once upon a time, there was a boy named Jack, and he loved to eat.

He ate everything his mother fed him, and because his mother loved Jack so much, she fed him anything he wanted.

As a result, he was literally eating her out of house and home. It was costing her a fortune.

So one day, she said, "Jack, take Hortense, our poor old cow, to the market and have her butchered so that I can make you more steaks."

Jack went off with Hortense, but he felt bad about having her killed so that he could eat her.

As he led Hortense slowly to the butcher shop in town, he met a man carrying a large sack over his shoulder, who looked all around as if to make sure no one was looking.

"Psst, hey kid, come over here," the man said out of the side of his mouth.

Intrigued, Jack led the cow over into an alley. "Hey, kid, have you ever seen any magic beans?" the man asked. Jack had not. Slowly, the man opened the bag to reveal all kinds of beans -- some red, some green, some black, some brown, some big, some small.

"These are magic beans, kiddo," he said. "All you gotta do is put two cups of 'em in six quarts of water, bring to a boil, and simmer for three hours." He paused.

"It don't hurt to add a little fried onion and garlic and maybe some of them little jars of tomato paste," he added. "Throw in your favorite spices, and it makes the best bean soup you ever tasted -- and it will also make you rich."

Jack, who wasn't very bright, thought this sounded great. After the man promised to keep Hortense as a pet, Jack traded the cow for the beans.

Then he went home and made the soup with some of the beans, while his mother was out tending their huge garden.

Jack ate a bowl. It was
fantastic!

He cut a big hunk of bread and dipped it into his second bowl, which was even better than the first.

After the third bowl, though, he couldn't eat any more.

"Burp!" said Jack, and he sat heavily in the armchair, where he fell asleep.

An hour later, Jack woke up in great discomfort. His stomach was growling and moving as if some animal were crawling around in it. With a loud flapping sound, he relieved some of the pressure through his behind.

The smell, even to Jack, was overwhelming. His mother, who was just coming in from outside, met Jack as he bolted outdoors.

Overcome with the odor, she too retreated.

"Jack, what in the world have you been eating now?" she asked, holding her nose.

"Magic (*fart*) bean (*poot*) soup (*phszzz*)," he said. "Look, I've got most of the beans left." He showed her the bag and explained how he had traded the cow for the beans.

"Jack, sometimes you drive me crazy!" his mother said. "Give me those beans. They're horrible. I'll throw them out."

"Nothing doing," Jack said, backing away, holding his bag of beans protectively. "That soup is delicious, and besides, eating it is going to make me rich. The man said so. It's too bad it gives me a little gas, though," he said, farting all the while.

Over the next hour, Jack's flatulence got worse and worse, so powerful that it began to propel him around the back yard.

In order to stay put, Jack tried lying on his back, but the gas blasted him up into the air, still holding his bag of beans, higher and higher, until he found himself passing through the clouds, up and up.

Finally a break in the stomach action left him lying on his back on a cloud in front of a huge castle.

Jack got up just in time for another blast of air from his behind to push him through the castle gate…

…where he bumped into a huge, soft expanse that turned out to be a giant's stomach.

"Oof!" said the giant, and he picked Jack up carefully by the back of his shirt. Jack spun around in a circle as the air hooshed from his butt. The giant, smelling the results, quickly put him down.

"Agh!" the giant said. "What's that horrible smell? Fe fi fo fum, I smell something just like scum. You smell worse than the day Uncle Art ate that huge helping of moose turd pie. And where did you come from, anyway?"

The terrified Jack explained that he had flown up from the earth, and that it was all because of the magic bean soup that would make him rich. The giant suddenly became very polite. "Oh, really? Let me take a look at those beans."

It turned out that the giant was a selfish giant who hoarded gold, diamonds and other jewels, along with a goose that laid golden eggs.

The giant loved magic things that produced wealth. Reluctantly, Jack handed over his sack of beans.

The giant was delighted, humming away as he cooked up all the beans according to Jack's directions. Then, in one gulp, he downed the entire batch. "Best bean soup I ever had," he said, and he burped.

Well, you know what
happened an hour later.

But in the case of the giant, the results were even more impressive, driving him out of his own castle. He flew around the heavens, but the resulting smell was anything but heavenly, and the sound of his gigantic flatulence was deafening.

Angels fled in every direction (some say this is when Lucifer came to earth).

Over the din, Jack could hear the giant crying out, "Fe fi fo fart, I smell as bad as Uncle Art," and other such anguished cries.

Jack wasted no time in grabbing the goose that laid the golden eggs and filling a bag with diamonds and jewels.

Then he jumped off the cloud and, using his gas supply to slow his fall (something like retro-rockets), he gently descended to earth again, landing beside his mother in the garden.

They lived happily ever after. Jack continued to issue horrendous-smelling gas from his rear end periodically for the rest of his life, but his mother forgave him, since the goose kept laying golden, non-odiferous eggs. They bought another cow and never lacked for food or anything else again.

And every time there was a big thunderstorm, Jack smiled to himself, knowing that it was his old friend the giant, who was still afflicted by his huge helping of magic bean soup.

<The End>

Breinigsville, PA USA
29 August 2010
244486BV00001B/2/P